D0130635

Dogsbottom School
Loses the Plot

Cavan County Library
Withdrawn Stock

Other books in the series

I Rule Dogsbottom School

Dogsbottom School Goes Totally Mental

Dogsbottom
School Loses
the Plot

Jon Blake

Illustrated by Sarah Nayler

OXFORD
UNIVERSITY PRESS

CAVAN COUNTY LIBRARY
ACC No.
CLASS No.
INVOICING
PRICE

OXFORD
UNIVERSITY PRESS

Great Clarendon Street, Oxford OX2 6DP

Oxford University Press is a department of the University of Oxford.
It furthers the University's objective of excellence in research, scholarship,
and education by publishing worldwide in

Oxford New York

Auckland Cape Town Dar es Salaam Hong Kong Karachi
Kuala Lumpur Madrid Melbourne Mexico City Nairobi
New Delhi Shanghai Taipei Toronto

With offices in

Argentina Austria Brazil Chile Czech Republic France Greece
Guatemala Hungary Italy Japan Poland Portugal Singapore
South Korea Switzerland Thailand Turkey Ukraine Vietnam

Oxford is a registered trade mark of Oxford University Press
in the UK and in certain other countries

Text copyright © Jon Blake 2005
Illustration copyright © Sarah Nayler 2005

The moral rights of the author and illustrator have been asserted

Database right Oxford University Press (maker)

First published 2005

All rights reserved. No part of this publication may be reproduced,
stored in a retrieval system, or transmitted, in any form or by any means,
without the prior permission in writing of Oxford University Press,
or as expressly permitted by law, or under terms agreed with the appropriate
reprographics rights organization. Enquiries concerning reproduction
outside the scope of the above should be sent to the Rights Department,
Oxford University Press, at the address above

You must not circulate this book in any other binding or cover
and you must impose this same condition on any acquirer

British Library Cataloguing in Publication Data
Data available

ISBN-13: 978-0-19-275395-3
ISBN-10: 0-19-275395-9

1 3 5 7 9 10 8 6 4 2

Printed in Great Britain by
Cox & Wyman Ltd, Reading, Berks.

CAVAN COUNTY LIBRARY

ACC No. C/206633

CLASS NO. J 9-11

INVOICE NO 7276 IES

PRICE €6.78

/ / JAN 2007

CONTENTS

CONTENTS

Invasion of the Aliens

I struggled for air. Miss Dorrit's knee was in my ribs and Mrs Whiffy's elbow was squashing my face like a beanbag. There was a minging smell—possibly the musty old books I was sitting on, but probably Mr Zinn's armpits. Counting Mr Stains, Mr Tomsky, Mrs Floss, and Moonbeam Jones, there were eight of us in the stock cupboard.

'Are they still there, Miss Dorrit?' hissed Mrs Whiffy.

Miss Dorrit peered through the little air vent

1

at the top of the cupboard. 'Afraid so, Mrs Whiffy,' she replied.

There was a ring on the school doorbell.

'Darn it!' hissed Mrs Whiffy. 'Everybody silent!'

The bell rang again.

'Will they never give up?' growled Mrs Whiffy.

Every week it was the same. Ever since Dogsbottom Primary had become a school for problem pupils, the Trumpshire Trouble Truck had arrived every Monday at 9 a.m. So far, however, not one problem pupil had made it through the front door. That was because Mrs Whiffy locked the door at five to nine precisely, just before she turned off all the lights and herded the entire school into the stock cupboard.

I wasn't complaining. I was quite happy that there were only two pupils at Dogsbottom Primary: yours truly (Bernie Lee), and my best mate Moonbeam.

Somehow, however, I knew it couldn't last.

'Mrs Whiffy!' gasped Miss Dorrit. 'We've left a window open!'

'*What?*' hissed Mrs Whiffy. 'Have they seen it?'

'They're climbing through it,' replied Miss Dorrit.

Everyone's eyes fell on Mr Tomsky, the caretaker. 'It was only open a crack!' he gibbered. 'For the school cat, see?'

Mrs Whiffy's fury was cut short as footsteps clacked down the corridor. 'Nobody breathe!' she croaked.

I quickly took one last deep breath, but it was a fatal mistake. I caught a double lungful of Mr Zinn's rancid armpits, and before I could stop it, a full-strength YEURRRRGH! had escaped my lips.

A few seconds of pure suspense followed.

With a slow creak, the stockroom door opened.

There stood Mr Graham Cloudy of Trumpshire County Council.

'Right!' said Mrs Whiffy, brightly. 'That's the end of assembly. Bernie, you stay behind to tidy up the hymn books.'

The staff clambered out, red-faced, as Mr Cloudy's brow furrowed.

'I do hope the hall floor's been mended by tomorrow!' said Mrs Whiffy. 'Now, can I help at all?'

'I have some new pupils for you,' said Mr Cloudy.

'Oh really,' said Mrs Whiffy, coldly.

'They're waiting at the entrance,' said Mr Cloudy.

Mr Cloudy led the way back towards the school door. Mrs Whiffy dragged her feet behind him, and I followed at a safe distance.

Nothing prepared us for the sight we were about to see.

'W-what are they?' asked Mrs Whiffy.

'Problem pupils,' replied Mr Cloudy.

'But . . . what kind of problem pupils?' asked Mrs Whiffy.

'Pupils who have been expelled from school,' replied Mr Cloudy.

'What kind of school turns out pupils like *that*?' asked Mrs Whiffy.

Mr Cloudy made no reply. Mrs Whiffy scanned the dozen or so children in front of her with a look of growing alarm on her face. The boy in front was wearing a *cravat*. The girl next to him was wearing a *feather boa*. The boy or girl

behind them had a white clown face and was trying to get out of an invisible box.

'Mrs Whiffy, I presume,' said the cravat boy, suddenly, with a princely bow. 'Redvers Grunt at your service . . . formerly of the Gertrude Mancini School of Dance, Drama, and the Performing Arts.'

I'd never thought Mrs Whiffy was religious, but at this point I distinctly saw her make the sign of the cross.

The Death of Larry Bedstain and Other Dramatic Events

Miss Dorrit, of course, was over the moon. She had a fresh flock of lovely pet lambs, and as she made up her register, she smiled wetly at the sound of each new name. There were twelve new pupils in all, but, like chocolates, too many at once may make you sick. I shall therefore offer you a selection:

BERNIE LEE'S GALLERY OF HORRORS
DO NOT ENTER IF OF A NERVOUS NATURE:

REDVERS GRUNT

Born at the age of 50. Planned to direct the Royal Shakespeare Company as soon as he left school, or possibly before. Always spoke as if full of enormous importance and wisdom, even when asking to go to the toilet.

TALOOLA STARR

Obviously liked to be the centre of attention 24/7 and then some. High arched eyebrows (possibly false) and a killer stare. Could tapdance before she could walk (so she said).

FLORIBEL FUNG

Delicate girl whose face and body were always going into twittery fits. Like a piece of litter in the wind. Felt you had to whisper when you were near her. Played piano to grade 950 or something.

LARRY BEDSTAIN

Mass of black curls and a face like a big soppy dog. Always looked like he was about to cry.

MILES BLACK

Punk hairstyle, long stripey scarf, and a face like a bored duck. I think he was supposed to be some kind of rebel. The kind that listens to weird indie bands then does what he's told.

If anything could scare off the new kids it was Mr Zinn. Mr Zinn was taking us for football first lesson. As you may know, Mr Zinn is a very intense person who gets very, very worked up about things but isn't very good at letting his feelings out. He's a bit like a boiling saucepan under a concrete lid. Coming across Mr Zinn could be very frightening to new pupils, with any luck.

As usual, Mr Zinn appointed two captains and asked them to pick teams. Normally this didn't take long as the only pupils were me and Moonbeam. Today, however, there were fourteen of us, and Redvers and Taloola were captains.

'Miles,' said Redvers. 'I shall audition you first.'

Mr Zinn looked worried but didn't seem to know what to say.

'I am Pele!' cried Miles, leaping into a dramatic pose. 'Greatest footballer in history!'

It gets worse.

'Dare you try to take the ball from me?' cried Miles, jumping into a new pose. 'I think not! Behold, the sheer nerve as I clip the goalie from the halfway line! Go-o-o-o-al!'

'OK, thank you, thank you,' said Redvers. 'You're in.'

Games time slowly ticked away as one audition followed another. Redvers actually called one person back twice because he wasn't sure about them. Taloola took even longer. I waited impatiently with Moonbeam, since we both seemed to be invisible.

Finally I got the call. It was Taloola. She looked me up and down with a cold, calculating stare. 'And what can you do?' she asked.

'I'm a goalie,' I replied.

'Goalie . . .' muttered Taloola, studying her team-sheet. 'No, we don't have any call for goalies. What else can you do?'

'Such as?' I growled.

'The piano,' replied Taloola. 'What can you do on the piano?'

'Piano?' I spluttered. 'What's that got to do with football?'

'It is a well-known fact,' said Taloola, 'that ability on the piano is a good guide to general character. Now, what can you do on the piano?'

I thought about this. 'I climbed on one once, to open a window,' I replied.

Taloola stared blankly at me for a while, then turned to Moonbeam. 'I'll have you,' she said.

I was hopping mad by the time we started to play. I wouldn't say I'm a *dirty* player, but I do like to get stuck in, and it wasn't long before Floribel Fung was having twittery fits just at the sight of me. But I swear I made *no contact whatsoever* with Larry Bedstain when we went for that fifty–fifty ball. Why he went sprawling I've no idea. Needless to say, Mr Zinn was soon surrounded by outraged children demanding a penalty with Oscar-winning speeches.

Larry, meanwhile, hadn't moved. Realizing this, Taloola rushed to his side. 'Come on, Larry,' she said. 'You can pull through.'

'Is that you, Taloola?' muttered Larry.

Taloola took Larry's hand.

'Guess I kinda messed up,' said Larry.

'No, Larry,' said Taloola, fighting back the tears. 'You did fine. Just fine.'

'Taloola,' mumbled Larry, 'if I don't make it, win this one for the Bedstain, eh?'

Larry made a weak effort to raise his head, then slumped back to the ground. Taloola's head rose, eyes misted with tears, a look of burning determination on her face.

'Is he all right?' asked Mr Zinn.

'Does he look all right?' fumed Taloola.

'Come on now, son,' said Mr Zinn. 'Get up.'

Larry lay still for another ten seconds or so, then jumped to his feet. 'That hurt,' he said.

At this point Mr Zinn blew his whistle. Not one shot on goal, and games time was over.

Funnily enough, Larry didn't seem to have any bad feelings towards me after the incident. In fact, he singled me out at lunchtime and told me he'd written a song for me. He said he'd never met a girl quite like me and the way he said it worried me. I didn't like big soppy dogs at the best of times, and I certainly didn't want one following me around all day at school.

'There's a piano in the hall,' said Larry. 'I could sing it now for you, if you like.'

'I think they're still having dinners in there,' I said quickly.

'No, everyone's out in the playground,' said Larry. 'It'll be just you and me.'

I swallowed hard.

'Come along, Bernie!' said Larry, opening the hall doors for me.

I suppose I could have made a run for it. But I did feel a bit guilty about almost breaking his leg, and besides, I had never had a song written for me before. I was slightly curious about it.

Larry sat himself at Mrs Whiffy's ancient piano and took a deep breath. I stood a safe distance away. Larry's hands came down to caress the old worn-down keys, his mouth opened, and out came a plaintive bleat:

'Simple person, living so fancy-free!

How I wish the whole wide world could see what I see!

Though you're short and stunted, in my eyes you're tall!

Though your face is plain, your soul is beautiful!'

Larry's hands died on the keys. His head slumped a little. He shook himself and turned shyly towards me.

'That's as far as I've got,' he said. 'Where do you think I should take it from here?'

'How about that little round basket in the corner of the room?' I suggested.

Larry's face fell. He seized his music and fled from the room. Well, honestly! What did he expect? I'm not short! Mum says I'm tall for a girl of my size. And besides, my soul is pig ugly, as Larry would soon find out, if he pestered me any more.

It really was time for a good moan with Moonbeam, which was what I did every lunch-time, even before the new kids arrived. I made my way out to the playground, where I found Moonbeam sitting on the wall by the bins.

But Moonbeam was not alone.

Taloola Starr was braiding her hair.

Outrage! I stormed back into school and headed straight for Mrs Whiffy's office. Braiding the hair of someone else's best friend was against school rules. At least it would be, once I'd had a word with Mrs Whiffy.

Unfortunately, however, Mrs Whiffy was already busy. She had decided to have an Afternoon Assembly and was helping Mr Tomsky to carry chairs into the hall. As soon as she saw me, she roped me in to help.

'Please, Miss,' I said. 'I've got some complaints about the new kids.'

'We're just going to have to make the best of it,' sniffed Mrs Whiffy. 'They're on the register and that's that.'

'But, Miss!' I pleaded. 'They're awful!'

'They're just *different*,' said Mrs Whiffy.

There was no point in arguing. Mrs Whiffy was talking like a teacher, not a normal person. We set out the chairs then sent Miss Dorrit out to ring the bell. Miss Dorrit always rang the bell these days as Mr Stains couldn't lift it any more.

The new kids were really up for assembly. That was because assembly meant singing, and singing meant showing off.

'Please, Miss,' suggested Redvers, 'instead of the hymn, could we do "You've Got To Pick a Pocket or Two" from *Oliver*? You could give a talk afterwards, just to say it isn't really right to pick pockets.'

15

'Just sit down, Redvers,' said Mrs Whiffy.

'Or I could give the talk, if you like,' suggested Redvers.

'Redvers,' said Mrs Whiffy, 'sit down.'

Mrs Whiffy was getting slightly aggravated, which was good news, as far as I was concerned. But she cheered up when the singing started, because it was the first time anyone apart from Miss Dorrit had actually sung at assembly. Soon it was time for Mrs Whiffy to read from her invisible book, the book called *1001 Incredibly Boring Talks That No One Ever Listens To*. Amazingly, the new kids *did* listen, or acted as if they were listening, and even listened to Announcements Time afterwards. Miss Dorrit announced a school trip to Dingley Dell Model Village, Mr Zinn announced the next school football game, and Mr Stains announced he'd fallen asleep with a loud snore.

Assembly was almost over, everything had gone smoothly, and I was feeling quite depressed.

Then Mrs Whiffy announced an item of lost property.

'A bus pass has been found,' she said, holding up a bus pass. 'Has anyone lost a bus pass?'

Suddenly there was a shriek from the back of the hall. Floribel Fung clapped her hands to her mouth, then leapt up and shook hands with everyone around her. She half-walked, half-ran to the stage, making twittery adjustments to her hair as she did so. Finally she bounded up to Mrs Whiffy, kissed her on the cheek, seized the bus pass and held it on high.

'I really wasn't expecting this!' she squealed. 'I haven't even got a speech prepared!'

There was a titter of laughter. Floribel took a deep breath and composed herself.

'I'd like to thank my mum and dad . . .' she began, '. . . Mrs Whiffy, of course, and all the other teachers . . . my agent, Rolf Pendleton . . . Amber Jessop, who does my hair . . .'

'OK, Floribel,' said Mrs Whiffy. 'That'll do.'

But Floribel was far from finished. She had only just started on a list slightly longer than the Bible. Despite all Mrs Whiffy's best efforts, she could not shut

Floribel up. And when Floribel did finally get to her final thank-you, to all of us out there, it was time for the waterworks to start. First a deep, soul-shuddering sigh, then a full-on, shoulder-shaking sob. Twittery hands dabbed a twittery hanky. Broken bits of thank-you sputtered into the air like dandelion seeds. Floribel Fung was overcome.

By the time Floribel was finally led away, and the hall had emptied, Mrs Whiffy looked a broken woman.

'They're just *different*, Mrs Whiffy,' I said.

Mrs Whiffy eyed me like a cornered animal. 'Bernie,' she said, 'I've got some homework for you.'

'Homework, Miss?' I repeated.

'I want you to make me a plan,' said Mrs Whiffy. 'A plan to rid me of these monsters for good.'

A Daring Plan and Then Another One

There were two great things about Moonbeam. One was her weird way of looking at things. The other was that she did everything I said. For instance, every Monday evening I held my doctor's surgery. Moonbeam never failed to turn up with a sick doll or injured teddy, and even though they usually died, she hardly ever complained.

Today, of course, was Monday, and Moonbeam turned up at 7 p.m. precisely at the Village Hall playing fields, second bench on the left, with a very poorly woolly poodle.

'Won't keep you a moment, Mrs Jones,' I said. I finished off some important paperwork then looked up over my imaginary glasses. 'Now, what seems to be the problem?'

'It's Fido,' replied Moonbeam. 'He won't eat.'

'Hmm,' I said. 'Is there a rash?'

'Hard to know,' replied Moonbeam. 'He's covered in fur.'

I gave Fido a doctor-type smile. 'Right, young man,' I said. 'Pop your top off and we'll have a listen to your chest.'

Fido didn't actually have a top to pop off, but I did have my plastic stethoscope, which was soon hard at work.

'Hmm,' I said. 'Nothing much the matter there. Let's just have a look at your tonsils.'

Fido didn't actually have tonsils either, but I pressed my lolly stick against his mouth and Moonbeam said Aah for him.

'Hmm,' I said. 'Mrs Jones, I'm afraid we'll have to operate.'

Moonbeam was most surprised. Usually it was just the rose-petal water three times a day till they stopped breathing.

'What's wrong with him?' she asked.

'He's got a lentil lodged in his soffagus,' I informed her.

'Are you sure?' said Moonbeam.

I placed my hands on my hips and fixed Moonbeam with a furious stare. 'Mrs Jones!' I rasped. 'Are you questioning my judgement as a doctor?'

'No, doctor,' peeped Moonbeam.

'I told you to feed him proper dogfood!' I barked.

'Sorry, doctor,' said Moonbeam.

'I'll just ring the hospital,' I said, pulling out my mobile phone. 'Hello? Is that the hospital? I need an appointment for an operation. Thank you.' I switched off the phone. 'Tomorrow evening, 7 p.m.,' I said.

Moonbeam looked doubtful. We'd never done operations before. But after ninety-five episodes of Doctors and Nurses I was keen to move on.

'You can be the nurse,' I whispered. 'You give me the swab and stuff.'

Moonbeam still looked doubtful.

'Oh, I know!' I said. 'You be the neesatist! You give him the gas!'

Moonbeam couldn't understand what I

meant, but she could see I was excited about it, so she got excited too. Now was the time to mention the other business of the evening.

'Moonbeam,' I said, 'I'll tell you a secret, but you're not allowed to tell anyone, not even your mum.'

Moonbeam nodded. Secrets were great, whatever they were.

'Moonbeam,' I said, 'I'm on a mission. And I want you to help.'

Moonbeam looked worried. 'It's not another crop circle, is it?' she asked. 'Cos my mum said—'

'Moonbeam,' I said, 'we've got to take out the stage kids.'

Moonbeam was puzzled. 'Take out?' she said. 'To the pictures, you mean?'

'No!' I protested. 'Not that kind of take out! The kind of take out that gangsters do!'

Moonbeam was even more confused. Her mum never let her watch gangster movies and she didn't even own a staple gun.

'Mrs Whiffy,' I explained, 'wants rid of the new kids. We have to come up with a plan to rub them out.'

'Rub them out?' repeated Moonbeam. 'But why?'

'Because they're a pain in the you-know-what,' I said.

'I like them,' said Moonbeam.

At the sound of these three little words, my whole world seemed to come to a halt. I had never had a row with Moonbeam, not a *real* row, but we would surely have one soon if she didn't change her tune.

'Oh, so you *enjoyed* Miss Princess Show-off doing your hair!' I snapped.

'What's that got to do with anything?' pleaded Moonbeam.

'I saw you,' I growled.

'I'm allowed to have my hair done, if I want,' said Moonbeam.

'It looks stupid,' I said.

Moonbeam's sensitive little face went all hurt. 'I like it,' she said.

'It's the kind of hairdo *they* would have,' I sneered.

'So what?' said Moonbeam. 'I think they're fun.'

'Moonbeam,' I stormed, 'they are *not* fun. They are *sad*.'

'I think they're fun,' repeated Moonbeam, quietly.

There was no point in continuing the conversation. I tramped off home in a simmering sulk. *What kind of thanks is this?* I asked myself. *What kind of thanks is this, when you teach a person how to have a mind of their own, then they start disagreeing with you!*

Luckily I am quite capable of making plans without help from Moonbeam. In fact, as I told myself next morning, I made better plans without her. She was always saying this was wrong, and that was wrong, and you can't hurt trees, and you must think of the *environment*, and you've got to be true to your *inner self*, and you shouldn't run people down in a combine harvester. She kind of cramped my style, if you know what I mean.

Mrs Whiffy, on the other hand, was much more ruthless than me, and greeted me at her office with eager eyes. 'Have you done your homework?' she asked.

'You know me, Mrs Whiffy,' I replied.

'Shut the door behind you,' said Mrs Whiffy.

I sauntered into Mrs Whiffy's room, slouched back in the chair and helped myself to a toffee. Luckily Mrs Whiffy's revolting aniseed balls had mysteriously disappeared some time back. Mrs Whiffy had never found out what actually happened to them, but I *had* noticed a strange aniseedy smell on Mr Tomsky's breath.

Outside we could hear cries of 'Avast, ye landlubbers!' and a distant chorus of 'Who will buy this wonderful morning?' Mrs Whiffy shuddered. 'What's the plan, Bernie?' she asked.

'It's like this, Mrs Whiffy,' I began. 'We paint a

big white cross on the school gates. Then we put up a sign: NO ENTRY—BLACK DEATH PLAGUE. Mr Tomsky puts Mr Stains on a cart—'

'Hold it right there, Bernie,' said Mrs Whiffy.

'What's the matter, Miss?' I replied.

'The last outbreak of black death plague,' said Mrs Whiffy, 'was in 1665.'

'Are you sure, Miss?' I asked. 'Didn't Joseph Button have it?'

'That was mumps,' replied Mrs Whiffy.

I was gutted. 'We could put NO ENTRY—MUMPS,' I suggested. 'But it wouldn't sound the same.'

Out in the playground, 'Who will buy this wonderful morning?' had come to an end, quickly replaced by 'Showbusiness is in my veins'.

'I can't take much more of this,' said Mrs Whiffy.

'How did they *ever* get thrown out of stage school?' I wondered. 'They're showbiz crazy!'

A puzzled look came over Mrs Whiffy. 'That's a good point, Bernie,' she said. 'Why *did* they get thrown out?'

'They're problem pupils *here*,' I said, 'but they wouldn't be problem pupils *there*.'

'They'd be perfect pupils *there*,' said Mrs Whiffy.

'Maybe there's something else about them,' I suggested. 'Something we don't know about.'

'Such as?' asked Mrs Whiffy.

'Maybe they change at full moon,' I suggested.

'Maybe they turn into human beings,' muttered Mrs Whiffy.

'Let's get rid of them quick,' I said, 'before something terrible happens.'

Suddenly we noticed the singing had stopped. There was the sound of an engine. We went to the window just in time to see a gold Mercedes pulling in. Mrs Whiffy's face soured. 'It's Curlew,' she growled.

Mr Curlew, of course, was the head of Buttery St Crumpet village school, the school wth the heated swimming pool, and the skateboard park, and its own cinema. Once upon a time Dogsbottom School had looked down on Buttery St Crumpet, and Mrs Whiffy longed with all her heart for those days to return.

There was a knock at the door. Mrs Whiffy grunted, 'Come!' and Mr Curlew entered, grinning broadly, with a briefcase in one hand and a door handle in the other.

'Sorry, Mildred!' he boomed. 'Just came off in my hand.'

'I was getting it fixed today,' mumbled Mrs Whiffy.

Mr Curlew gazed around Mrs Whiffy's shabby old office with a self-satisfied smile. He was wearing a new cream suit and a designer Buttery St Crumpet tie. 'How are things at the old dump?' he said. 'I see you've got some new pupils.'

'Things are just fine, thank you,' grunted Mrs Whiffy.

'Did I tell you Jennifer Plummet was at my school now?' asked Mr Curlew. 'You know, the daughter of Julian Plummet, head of Plummet Airlines?'

'Yes, you did tell me,' muttered Mrs Whiffy. 'Several times.'

'I've had to ask him to stop sending us money,' said Mr Curlew. 'We really don't know what to do with it.'

'Do you have a *purpose* for this visit?' rasped Mrs Whiffy.

'Of course,' said Mr Curlew. He opened his briefcase, took out some posters, and laid them on Mrs Whiffy's desk. 'I was wondering if you could put these up,' he said.

We studied a poster:

**BUTTERY ST CRUMPET VILLAGE SCHOOL
PRESENTS THE SMASH HIT MUSICAL**

JOSEPH AND HIS AMAZING STAIN-RESISTANT JIMJAMS

May 1—3, 7p.m.
In the school's new
JULIAN PLUMMET THEATRE
Starring JENNIFER PLUMMET & others

**THE SCHOOL PLAY EVENT
OF THE YEAR!**

'Don't miss it!'— Buttey St Crumpet School Magazine

'I laughed till I cried'— Mrs Charlene Curlew

'Would you like me to reserve you a ticket?' asked Mr Curlew.

'No thank you,' replied Mrs Whiffy. 'I'm having my hair done that day.'

'The play's on for three days,' said Mr Curlew.

'I'm having my hair done the other two days as well,' replied Mrs Whiffy.

'Not to worry!' said Mr Curlew, brightly. 'We're sure to have a full house anyway. Well, I shall have to love you and leave you, Mildred.'

'Leaving me will be sufficient, thank you,' muttered Mrs Whiffy.

We watched Mr Curlew sail briskly away, then listened to the quiet purr of his Mercedes down the school drive.

'Now,' said Mrs Whiffy, looking round. 'Where shall I put these posters?' She carried the said posters calmly over to the swing-top bin by the window. 'I think *just here will be fine*,' she hissed, thrusting them inside with a sudden and quite scary force.

'He's a twit, that Mr Curlew,' I said.

Mrs Whiffy wasn't listening. She was pacing the room, deep in thought.

'If you give me the morning off,' I said, 'I'll come up with another plan.'

Mrs Whiffy came out of her private world. 'Plan?' she said. 'Plan for what?'

'To get rid of the new kids,' I reminded her.

Mrs Whiffy was aghast. 'Get rid of the new

kids?' she said. 'You must be joking!'

'Eh?' I gasped.

'I need every one of those kids,' said Mrs Whiffy. 'Those kids are going to put on a play. A play which will blow Curlew's puny musical right off the stage!'

A Helpless Rabbit Savaged
by a Puma

Later that day a new poster went up in school:

AUDITIONS
FOR
PETER PAN
This year's Dogsbottom School Play
3.30p.m. tomorrow School Hall

I doubt if any poster in history caused such drama. It was as if the cup final, Christmas dinner, and the world's favourite boy-band had all arrived at once. The new kids went totally mental. Within minutes of the poster going up, all the copies of *Peter Pan: the Junior Stage Edition* had disappeared from the school book store. By lunchtime everyone had decided what part they wanted and learnt at least half their lines. The trouble was, everyone wanted the same part as someone else, and the playground was full of show-offs duelling with each other, yelling stuff like, 'I can fly! Look, everybody, I can fly!'

'It's pathetic,' I said to Moonbeam.

Moonbeam said nothing.

'Moonbeam,' I grunted, 'don't tell me you want to be in this play.'

A look of vague pain and anxiety came over her. 'It looks like a laugh,' she said.

'No, Moonbeam,' I said. 'This is what a laugh looks like.' I opened my mouth like a horse and cackled like a witch.

Moonbeam ignored me. 'I'd *like* to have a go,' she said, 'but I just don't think I'd be good enough.' She gave me a sideways glance, a glance I knew very well. For the past three months I'd been constantly assuring Moonbeam she *could* do this, she *could* do that, she didn't need to fear *anyone*, and she should be ready for *anything*.

'What do you think?' Moonbeam peeped.

'You're right,' I assured her. 'You'd be rubbish.'

Moonbeam's face dropped. But the conversation was cut short by the breathless arrival of Larry. 'I've got it!' he said.

'Don't give it to us,' I replied.

'Peter!' he cried. 'I've got Peter!'

'Who says?' I asked.

'Redvers!' said Larry.

'Redvers isn't the director!' I scoffed. 'Mrs Whiffy is!'

Larry's eyes flashed shiftily from side to side. 'Yes,' he replied. 'I know that. But everyone listens to Redvers.'

'I don't,' I replied.

Larry came over sheepish. 'Have you thought . . .' he muttered, '. . . about going for Tinkerbell?'

'Yes,' I replied. 'I've thought about going for her with a combine harvester.'

Larry ignored my joke. 'I think you'd be great,' he said.

'You don't think I'd be too *simple*?' I asked.

'Why do you say that?' said Larry.

'Oh, I think I'd be *far* too simple,' I replied. 'Just look at the competition.'

There certainly was competition. All morning a row had been simmering between Taloola and Floribel. Needless to say, Taloola wanted to be Tinkerbell, but so did Floribel, which really annoyed Taloola, especially since Floribel had taken the lead in *Annie* when she *knew* Taloola wanted it but couldn't get back from her manicure in time for the audition.

The tension took its toll on Floribel. Around two o'clock she disappeared and we heard she'd gone home with a migraine. That left the way clear for Taloola, and come three-thirty she was out of the classroom door like a bolt of lightning. She was still behind me, mind, except I was on my way home.

At least I *thought* I was on my way home, till Mrs Whiffy collared me.

'Where do you think you're going, Bernie?'

'Don't want to be in the play thanks, Miss,' I replied.

Mrs Whiffy's eyes narrowed. 'I don't think you understand, Bernie,' she said. 'This is a *school* play. That means a play for the *whole school*.'

'But I can't act, Miss!' I protested.

'We need more than actors, Bernie,' said Mrs Whiffy. 'We need carpenters . . . costume designers . . .' Mrs Whiffy glanced at the book she was holding, which was *Play Staging For Beginners*. '. . . front of house managers . . . props managers . . . musical directors . . .'

'But I can't do those things either,' I protested.

'Nonsense,' replied Mrs Whiffy. 'Now follow me.'

I trudged miserably after Mrs Whiffy into the hall, where Moonbeam, the entire teaching staff, Mr Tomsky the caretaker, and Mrs Floss the school cook were sitting rigidly in their chairs. The new kids were pacing nervously about, and at the sight of Mrs Whiffy fought for places in a queue by the stage. Mrs Whiffy took a seat at the front of the hall, had another quick leaf through *Play Staging For Beginners*, then called for the first in the queue, which was Larry.

'Please, Miss,' said Larry, 'I want to read Peter.'

'I shall decide what you will read,' replied Mrs Whiffy. She opened *Peter Pan: the Junior Stage Edition* and considered carefully. 'I'd like you to do Act Two, Scene One, reading the part of . . . Peter.'

Mrs Whiffy offered Larry the book, but Larry was already away. 'But soft, what light through yonder window breaks!' he cried. 'It is the east, and Tinkerbell is the sun!'

'Hmm,' said Mrs Whiffy. 'I'm not sure . . .'

Mrs Whiffy stopped. She had become aware that someone was pacing up and down behind her. She turned to see Redvers, looking very serious and thoughtful, with his thumb under his chin and his pointy finger tapping softly against his nose.

'Can I help, Redvers?' asked Mrs Whiffy.

'Do you mind if I ask you a question?' asked Redvers.

'What is that, Redvers?' asked Mrs Whiffy.

'Mrs Whiffy,' began Redvers, 'how many plays have you directed?'

'Why do you ask that?' growled Mrs Whiffy.

'I've directed forty-two,' announced Redvers.

'And?' replied Mrs Whiffy.

'Forgive me saying,' said Redvers, 'but I get the distinct impression you don't know what you're doing, whereas I most certainly do.'

Mrs Whiffy reddened. 'May I remind you,' she said, 'that I am your headteacher.'

'Indeed,' said Redvers, 'and therefore not a director.'

Mrs Whiffy puffed up like a cobra. But just as she was about to strike, she seemed to have a change of mind. Maybe she was thinking of Buttery St Crumpet's play, and how desperately she wanted to outdo it. 'So, Redvers,' she said. 'You think you can do a better job, do you?'

'With respect, Mrs Whiffy,' replied Redvers, 'I know I can. But if you like, you can be my assistant director.'

Mrs Whiffy frowned. 'What would that involve?' she asked.

'Allow me to demonstrate,' said Redvers. He held out his briefcase. 'Could you just hold this a moment?' he asked.

Mrs Whiffy stood up, took the briefcase and waited. Nothing happened. 'I thought you were going to demonstrate what an assistant director does,' she said.

'I've just done that,' replied Redvers.

Mrs Whiffy looked down at the briefcase in her hand. 'This?' she said. 'This is all I do?'

'Oh no, far from it,' replied Redvers. 'Two sugars, please, and go easy on the milk.'

Mrs Whiffy's jaw dropped, and at that moment Redvers slipped into the director's chair. 'Thank you, Larry darling,' he said. 'You've got the part.'

Mrs Whiffy bristled for a few moments, checked to see if anyone was watching, then sat quietly in the chair behind.

'Next!' said Redvers.

Taloola strode onto the stage. 'Peter, Peter!' she boomed. 'Where are you, Peter?' She dropped to her knees and tried hard to squeeze out a tear.

'Hmm,' said Redvers. 'I see Tinkerbell as gentle and innocent. You're coming over a bit *tough*.'

In an instant Taloola went as weak and helpless as a sick rabbit. 'Peter!' she whimpered. 'Where *are* you, Peter?'

'Hmm,' said Redvers. 'Can you do the bit where you die?'

It was funny that Redvers said this, because it was exactly what I was thinking. But obviously it wasn't what Taloola wanted to do. She hummed and ha'd, mumbled, 'Oh, misery!' a few times, then gave a big dramatic sigh.

'Redvers,' she announced, 'I cannot do this scene without a wand.'

Redvers turned to Mrs Whiffy. 'Assistant?' he said.

Mrs Whiffy turned to me. 'Bernie?' she said.

'I don't think we're supposed to have wands in school,' I replied.

At this point Mr Tomsky piped up. 'I've got a small trowel in my potting shed,' he suggested. 'Will that do?'

'Thank you, Mr Tomsky,' said Mrs Whiffy 'Bernadette, get the small trowel from Mr Tomsky's potting shed.'

'It's right behind the gro-bags,' added Mr Tomsky, 'underneath the drag net.'

I wasn't complaining. Any excuse to get out of that hall. Anyway, I liked Mr Tomsky's potting shed. It was easily the most interesting place in school, full of tools and composts and instant death poisons. There was lots of fishing gear as well, like buoys and ropes and nets, because Mr Tomsky was once a fisherman, and kept all his stuff in case global warming turned Dogsbottom into an island. Sometimes he'd take me aside and give me useful little tips, like how to use a drag net to snare enough cod to feed the village.

Mr Tomsky's shed was on the far side of the school field, which was a nice long walk, especially at two miles an hour. About halfway across the field, however, I became aware of a noise. It was a strange, high-pitched whimpering. As I drew closer to the potting shed, so the noise got louder. My footsteps quickened. *I've heard that noise before!* I thought. *He's locked that stray dog in there again!*

With anxious hands I drew back the bolt on the door. 'It's all right, girl!' I cried, throwing open the door.

There before me, sitting on an upturned bucket, was a raging, tearful Floribel.

'*She* did this!' she cried.

I didn't bother asking who 'she' was, and I didn't have time, either. Floribel was past me in a flash, matchstick legs galloping towards the hall. Not wanting to miss the fun, I gave chase. I caught up just as Floribel was throwing open the hall doors. Up on stage, her mortal enemy stopped looking innocent and gentle, and started looking worried.

'I'll kill you!' screeched Floribel. She flew

towards the stage, scattering chairs, then pounced like a puma. The two would-be Tinkerbells went into a full-on, no-holds-barred playground brawl, except, of course, they weren't in the playground.

The teachers were too shocked to do anything. Only one person rushed in to break it up, and that was Moonbeam.

'Stop it!' she cried. 'Peace! Peace on Earth!'

Before everyone's astonished eyes, Moonbeam threw herself right between the two brawling girls, stopping them in their tracks. Her jaw was set firm and her eyes shone with the radiance of a saint.

The whole hall went silent. Then, slowly and dramatically, Redvers rose from his chair and placed his hand on his heart. 'Great heaven be praised!' he cried. 'I have found my Tinkerbell!'

A Galumphing Carthorse Meets the World's Worst Nurse

Seven o'clock had passed and the air was tense in Operating Theatre 3. Dr Lee was scrubbed up and ready in her green plastic gown with GARDEN REFUSE ONLY printed on the back. Fido Jones was waiting anxiously on the operating table, fully conscious seeing as SOMEONE hadn't turned up to give him his gas. SOMEONE was going to be in big trouble with the hospital authorities and could be paying a VERY NASTY FORFEIT.

Ah! At last! The always-on-time Moonbeam

Jones appeared in the distance, TEN MINUTES LATE.

A frosty silence awaited her.

'Didn't get home from school till six,' she explained.

'Really,' I replied. I didn't ask why, because I knew why, and I didn't want to mention anything about the school play audition. I preferred to pretend the stupid play wasn't happening, and Moonbeam had nothing to do with it.

'What have I got to do?' asked Moonbeam.

'Nurse Jones,' I replied. 'You should not have to ask *me* what to do. Now put the patient out and we'll get to work.'

Rather uncertainly, Moonbeam gave Fido a pretend injection. After giving it five seconds to take effect, I made the first incision.

'Swab,' I ordered.

'Clamp,' I ordered.

'Pliers,' I ordered.

I worked with quick nimble fingers, but this was a dangerous operation.

'Check the heartbeat,' I ordered.

Moonbeam took Fido's pulse.

'You're not with it, Nurse Jones!' I snapped. 'On the machine! The machine!'

Moonbeam looked clueless.

'All right, I'll be the machine!' I cried. 'Be-beep . . . be-beep . . . be-beep . . .'

'It's fine,' said Moonbeam.

'No it isn't!' I railed. 'It's too beepy!'

'Stop getting at me!' cried Moonbeam.

'I'm not getting at you!' I barked.

'Just cos I'm in the—' Moonbeam blurted.

'What?' I snapped.

'The play,' said Moonbeam.

Silence.

'Oh,' I hissed, 'so you're going to do it.'

'Of course I am,' said Moonbeam.

Silence.

'Taloola will *hate* you for being Tinkerbell,' I said.

'Actually,' replied Moonbeam, 'she's been very nice about it. She just didn't want Floribel to do it.'

'Oh yeah,' I scoffed. 'Well, Floribel will hate you, that's for sure!'

'Actually,' replied Moonbeam, 'Floribel's been nice too. She just didn't want Taloola to do it.'

Silence.

'Nurse Jones!' I cried. 'For Pete's sake, watch the patient!'

'All you do is tell me what to do,' muttered Moonbeam.

'Be-beep . . . be-beep . . . beeeeeeeeeeeeeeeeeeee-eeeeeeeeeeeeeeeeeeeeeee!' I cried. 'We've lost him!'

I picked up Fido by his foot. He dangled limply. 'Shall we play undertakers now?' I snapped.

'I've got more important things to do,' said Moonbeam.

With that, Moonbeam stuffed Fido into her bag and left. *She'll be back*, I said to myself. I was still saying it half an hour later, at which time I decided it was time to go home.

The first rehearsal for *Peter Pan* was timetabled for the next evening. We lost half our footy game because Mr Zinn was trying on his crocodile suit, and half our lunch because Mrs Floss was practising Third Pirate and had forgotten where she'd buried the sponge pudding. In the afternoon Miss Dorrit showed everyone the costumes she'd designed, and everyone went

OOOOOOOOOOOO and AAAAAAAAAAH when they saw the dress for Tinkerbell. It was a wispy sparkly feathery thing that Moonbeam would look SIMPLY GORGEOUS in, according to Taloola, who simply HAD to squeeze Moonbeam's hand in sheer delight.

Glumly, I watched everyone file into the hall after school. I had told Moonbeam that I'd have to operate on Fido again as I'd accidentally left my nail scissors inside him, but Moonbeam didn't seem to hear. Now that she was wrapped up in this stupid play fantasy, the real world didn't seem to matter any more.

Redvers was last into the hall. He was prowling across the foyer with a clipboard when he caught sight of me.

'Bernadette!' he cried. 'Don't you want to join our happy throng?'

'Happy what?' I said. 'Thong?'

'Throng!' cried Redvers. 'The people with parts! You could have a part, Bernadette! Don't you fancy being one of the Lost Children?'

'I'd rather be a lost *dog* than be in your play,' I replied. With that I tramped out of school, and set off for home the long way, across the muddy fields. My shoes went SHLOP and GLOP in the wet clay, but I didn't care. I had lost my best friend to *Peter Pan* and muddy shoes didn't matter.

As I stood on Moonsticks bridge, I couldn't face going home. I was thinking of the nature rambles I used to have with Moonbeam, and how she'd taught me to make woodman's tea out of birch sap and pine needles. She knew lots of stuff like that, Moonbeam, even if she couldn't put on her jumper the right way round.

But I was not defeated yet. One way or another, I would get Moonbeam out of that stupid play and away from those stupid stage school kids.

But how?

At this point, Plan A came into my head. I would visit Moonbeam's mum, and warn her about the terrible things which would happen to her daughter if she went ahead with this play. Maybe Moonbeam wouldn't listen to me any more, but she was sure to listen to her mum, because her mum was queen of the earth or something. She was in touch with important stuff—something to do with ley-lines which run up your legs and give you headaches.

I rang Moonbeam's doorbell with a slight sense of dread. I was never sure what Mrs Jones would be doing, but it was rarely anything normal. Sure enough, there she was, through the hall window, dancing clumsily about, fanning the air with scarves. I had obviously chosen a bad day, but just as I began to creep away, the door was flung open.

'Do I spy the Wicker Child?' cried Mrs Jones.

I stopped dead. 'It's Bernie,' I replied. Mrs Jones knew this very well, but seemed to find it impossible to use my real name.

'Would you like to dance with me, Wicker Child?' asked Mrs Jones.

My blood froze. 'Er...' I muttered.

'Come!' cried Mrs Jones, ushering me inside, then continuing with her mad gypsy dance. The house smelt of musk oil and boiled beetroot, and there was not a stereo in sight.

'Where's the music?' I asked.

'Can't you hear it?' cried Mrs Jones, cupping a hand to her ear.

I shook my head.

'You must be a Gemini,' said Mrs Jones.

This was getting embarrassing. Not having much choice, I hopped gently from one foot to another, although I did at least do this in rhythm. Mrs Jones didn't seem too bothered about rhythm. If you could cross a galumphing carthorse with a fairy, that would be Moonbeam's mum.

'They used to laugh at me dancing at school,' cried Mrs Jones. 'They don't laugh now!'

That's because they're not here, I thought to myself.

'Please, Mrs Jones,' I said, 'I need to talk to you about Moonbeam.'

Mrs Jones stopped dead. Her face was full of panic. 'Has something happened to her?' she gasped.

'Yes,' I replied. 'She's been given a part in the school play.'

Mrs Jones breathed a sigh of relief. 'Oh, that,' she said. 'I know about that.'

'You're not worried?' I asked.

'Should I be?' asked Mrs Jones.

'In my opinion,' I replied, 'yes.'

Mrs Jones looked worried again. 'You'd better come through to the kitchen and have a cup of tea,' she said.

We walked down the hall, past fifteen jars of assorted buttons, into the kitchen, with ten zillion jars of assorted beans. I sat on a wicker chair by a giant peasant table while Mrs Jones put on the kettle.

'Nettle, Hibiscus, or Camomile?' trilled Mrs Jones.

'Have you got any Ty-phoo?' I asked.

'I've got my Special Dogsbottom Mix,' replied Mrs Jones.

'OK,' I said. 'I'll have that.'

Ah well, I thought. It's all in the cause of duty. Mrs Jones placed a big lumpy mug of steaming grey-green water in front of me and I took a sip. 'Mm,' I said. 'This is well named.'

'How do you mean?' asked Mrs Jones, frowning.

'I mean it's special,' I replied.

Mrs Jones smiled. 'I'm so glad you think so,' she said. She sounded kind of false, but then she always did. 'Now, what is the problem with Moonbeam?'

I put on a look of grave concern, like a newsreader about to announce a disaster. 'It's too much for her,' I said.

'What is too much?' asked Mrs Jones.

'The words,' I replied. 'She's got too many words to learn.'

'Moonbeam is a very good learner,' said Mrs Jones.

'Yes, but she's got no time to do her maths!' I said. 'Or her history! Or . . . her country dancing!'

Mrs Jones was not convinced. 'I'm sure Mrs Whiffy will make sure she gets her work done,' she said.

I shook my head. 'Mrs Whiffy,' I said, 'is a maniac.'

Mrs Jones laughed.

'Seriously!' I said. 'She's obsessed with putting on a better play than Buttery St Crumpet, and she'll stop at nothing to do it!'

Mrs Jones still wasn't convinced. Like most parents, she thought headteachers were normal, responsible people. She'd never seen Mrs Whiffy climbing up the school tower with a stick of dynamite. I had, but that's another story.

'You're not drinking your tea,' she said.

I held my breath and knocked it back. My plan wasn't working. I needed to try another angle. 'There is another problem,' I said, even more gravely.

'In that case,' said Mrs Jones, 'we'd better have some cake.'

Before I could stop her, Mrs Jones had pulled down a round wicker box, taken out a big lump of Something, and cut me off a huge slice.

'It's Vegetable Seed Cake,' she explained.

I winced. The slice of cake was almost entirely made up of seeds, with a few lumps of carrot in between. I took a little nibble and swallowed quickly. 'There's this new girl,' I said. 'Her name's Taloola. She wanted to be Tinkerbell. She locked up another girl who wanted to be Tinkerbell, then beat her up.'

This time I'd scored a bull's-eye. 'That's terrible!' cried Mrs Jones.

'I'm really scared what she might do to Moonbeam,' I added.

'We must tell the teachers!' cried Mrs Jones.

'The teachers are scared of her,' I continued. 'She beat that girl up right in front of them.'

Mrs Jones stood up dramatically. 'I will not have Moonbeam within a hundred miles of this girl!' she announced.

'You better stop her doing the play then,' I said.

'I will ring the school this minute!' cried Mrs Jones. But just then, the latch went on the front door. Footsteps pattered down the hall. The kitchen door swung open, and there stood Moonbeam.

'Hi, Mummy,' said Moonbeam, with an anxious glance towards me. 'I've brought home my new friend.'

Moonbeam stood aside, and in walked Taloola Starr. 'Hello, Mrs Jones,' she trilled. 'I'm *so* pleased to meet you! What a *gorgeous* house!'

'Oh, thank you,' said Mrs Jones.

'Look what she's given me,' said Moonbeam. She fished in her bag and brought out a CD. 'It's a CD of the play. It'll be easy to learn my lines with this!'

'Oh, isn't that thoughtful!' said Mrs Jones.

'Moonbeam's a *fantastic* Tinkerbell,' said Taloola. 'I must admit I was *quite* jealous of her at first, but then I got the part of Wendy, and *actually* I think it's the best part in the play.'

'We've got loads of scenes together,' said Moonbeam.

'We're a great team,' added Taloola.

'Wonderful,' replied Mrs Jones. 'Moonbeam, aren't you going to introduce me properly to your new friend? I don't even know her name.'

'Sorry,' said Moonbeam. 'Mummy, this is Taloola.'

Taloola gave a wide warm smile. Mrs Jones looked gobsmacked. 'But . . . isn't she the *horrible* girl?' she asked.

'Who told you that?' asked Moonbeam.

Mrs Jones looked straight at me. I was like an animal backed into a corner, and like an animal, I came out fighting.

'Can't you see?' I cried, leaping up. 'She's not really nice! She's *acting*!'

For a moment there was an embarrassed silence. Then a twisted smile appeared on Taloola's lips. 'That's rich,' she said, 'coming from the girl who said that Moonbeam was rubbish.'

I stared in shock at Moonbeam. 'What d'you tell her that for?' I gasped.

'Why did you say it in the first place?' countered Moonbeam.

'It was a joke!' I said.

'It didn't sound like a joke,' said Moonbeam.

'It sounds like a *terrible* thing to say,' added Mrs Jones.

'What do you know, you . . . *hippy witch*!' I blurted.

An awful cold silence fell over the room. Moonbeam opened the door. 'Goodbye, Bernadette,' she said. 'I only invite *friends* into this house.'

Peter Pan's Greatest Fan Has To Make Another Plan

Next morning, when Moonbeam got to school, I was lying in wait for her. 'Hi, Moonbeam!' I said, cheerily.

Moonbeam did not seem to hear me.

'Moonbeam,' I continued, 'did you realize that witches were these really clever women who knew about herbs and stuff, and that's why they cooked witches with faggots?'

Moonbeam was not responding.

'So when I said your mum was a witch . . .' I began.

'Don't bother,' said Moonbeam. She sat on the steps by the school front doors, and took out her copy of *Peter Pan*.

'Learnt your lines yet?' I asked.

'What do you care?' muttered Moonbeam.

'It's a wicked idea, doing this play,' I said.

'Don't lie,' said Moonbeam.

'I mean it!' I protested. 'I'm all for it! I know I was a bit iffy about it before, but that was because I fell off stage in a nativity play once.'

Suddenly Moonbeam looked me straight in the eyes. 'If you're for this play,' she said, 'prove it. And until then, don't expect me to talk to you.'

She'll back down, I said to myself. *She'll* talk to me. I said it all through first lesson, then break, then lunch. But Moonbeam did not utter one word, except to teachers and her wonderful new friends. A sick feeling grew in the pit of my stomach, then climbed out of the pit and started to head up my throat. Life was suddenly terribly empty.

Slowly, painfully, the truth began to dawn on me. Moonbeam really would not speak to me again. Unless, of course, I proved I was Peter Pan's greatest fan.

And that meant—gulp—that I had to talk to Redvers.

'*Redvers*,' I began, 'you know when I said I didn't want to join your happy thong?'

'Throng,' replied Redvers. 'What about it?'

'I had a headache,' I explained.

'So?' said Redvers.

'I couldn't think straight,' I explained.

A secret smile flickered on Redvers's lips. 'Would you be after a part, Bernadette?' he asked, smirkily.

'Um . . . kind of,' I replied.

'Well,' said Redvers. 'This is an honour.'

'Are there any parts left?' I asked, meekly.

'Well, Bernadette,' replied Redvers. 'There is *one*.'

'What is it?' I asked.

'Nana,' replied Redvers.

'Nana?' I repeated.

'Nana,' repeated Redvers.

There was a short pause. 'OK,' I said. 'I'll do it.'

'You may audition for the part first thing after school,' said Redvers.

'Audition?' I repeated. 'What, in front of everyone?'

'That, my dear,' drawled Redvers, 'is rather the point of the *theatre*.'

Redvers tossed back an imaginary scarf and swanned away. He really was a twit.

Well, I thought to myself. We'll see who can act.

For the rest of the day I practised being a doddery old dear. It wasn't hard. I did a bit of dozing, and knitting, and cupping a hand to my ear. I walked with a trembly old hobble and talked with a quavery old warble. By the time four o'clock came round, the whole world would really think I *was* a doddery old dear, except about sixty years younger.

I marched straight into the hall, past Moonbeam, Miles, Mrs Whiffy, and the rest, and took my place boldly on stage, trying hard not to look at Taloola, who was also on stage and in the middle of a speech.

'Right!' I bellowed. 'What do you want me to do?'

Taloola fell silent. So did the whole hall. Redvers leant back in his director's chair and pointed to the space next to Taloola. 'Go over there,' he said.

I took a deep breath, marched across the stage and stood confidently next to Moonbeam's new best friend, yuck.

'Now let's see your Nana,' said Redvers.

I hunched myself up with one hand against my back. 'Oo!' I croaked. 'My old back! I could murder a cup of tea!'

'No, no, no, no, no!' cried Redvers.

'What's wrong with that?' I said.

'You're standing all wrong!' said Redvers.

'In what way?' I replied.

'You should be on all fours!' cried Redvers.

'On all fours?' I repeated.

'Just do it, please, dear,' said Redvers.

I really didn't take to being called 'dear', but I got down as instructed, trying hard not to look at Taloola towering above me. 'Have I lost my contact lenses?' I asked.

'Very funny,' said Redvers. 'Now beg.'

'What?' I gasped.

'Just do it, please, dear,' said Redvers.

This was getting more and more ridiculous. 'Got a few pence for a biscuit?' I warbled, holding out a quivery hand.

'No, no, no, no, no!' cried Redvers.

'What's wrong this time?' I snapped.

'You're talking!' cried Redvers.

'Of course I'm talking!' I replied. 'What else would I be doing?'

'Barking!' cried Redvers.

'Barking?' I repeated, more baffled than ever.

Redvers slapped a hand to his forehead. 'You do understand,' he said, 'that Nana is a dog?'

There was a moment's silence, while I took in this new and rather shocking piece of information. 'A dog?' I repeated.

'I thought *everyone* knew that,' proclaimed Redvers, and all the stage school kids tittered.

'What other parts are there?' I asked.

'No other parts,' replied Redvers. 'Just Nana.'

I considered again the thought of trotting doggedly behind Taloola for the next month. No, it wasn't looking any more attractive.

'I'll be assistant director,' I suggested.

'*I'm* assistant director!' cried Mrs Whiffy, leaping to her feet.

'Assistant assistant director then,' I suggested.

'We do not need an assistant assistant director!' snapped Mrs Whiffy. 'Do we, Redvers?' she added, anxiously.

'We do not,' confirmed Redvers. 'However . . . we do need a props manager.'

Props manager. That didn't sound too hard. All I'd have to do was fetch some swords and clocks and things.

'OK,' I said. 'I'll do it. What's my first job?'

'Your first job,' replied Redvers, 'is to make Peter Pan fly.'

I nodded thoughtfully.

'Any ideas how you might do that, Bernie?' asked Miss Dorrit.

I continued to nod thoughtfully. 'What I think I might do,' I suggested, 'is start with my second job.'

'Very well,' said Redvers.

'So,' I said, 'what is my second job?'

'To make Tinkerbell fly,' replied Redvers.

I glanced anxiously at Moonbeam, who was watching me with considerable interest. 'You're on,' I said.

The King of the Jungle and a Squeal of Tyres

Mum couldn't understand why I was working so hard on my homework. But I wasn't actually doing my homework. I was drawing designs of parachutes and catapults and small rocket packs that could be worn on your back beneath your sparkly wispy costume.

None of them were very convincing. Not even the super-magnet. For the super-magnet to work, Peter Pan would have to wear a suit of armour. I don't suppose that would look right, Peter Pan in a suit of armour. Even then, he'd shoot across the stage at two thousand miles an hour. If anyone was in his way they'd be toast.

The days began to pass, and every day someone would ask me how it was going. I'd say, 'Coming on, coming on', and they'd go, 'Yeah, right.' But I would show them.

Meanwhile, the rehearsals for *Peter Pan* were going fabulously. That was the word Redvers used, so it must have been true. Mr Zinn was particularly snappy as the crocodile, and Mrs Floss really stood out as Third Pirate, being a foot taller than all the other pirates. Taloola and Floribel were out-shouting each other nicely as Wendy and Tiger Lily, and Moonbeam was of course *adorable* as Tinkerbell. Tinkerbell's death scene was particularly moving. Larry Bedstain had cried all next day and was now in love with Moonbeam, which was a relief for me at least.

Mrs Whiffy was full of glee. She was sure the play would be a hit, so she started up the Publicity Machine. The Publicity Machine was actually Mrs Whiffy running off some posters and Miss Dorrit colouring them in, as the school couldn't afford a colour printer. But the posters did look quite striking, as Miss Dorrit liked bright primary colours and filled in the Os with little smiley faces. The teachers took some home, and soon the posters were appearing in the village post office, the village stores, the village hall, the village church, and the village surgery. There wasn't actually anything else in Dogsbottom, apart from the houses. But Mrs Whiffy had plans to advertise further afield.

'Come with me, Bernie,' she said. 'We're going to pay Mr Curlew a little visit.'

We set off for Buttery St Crumpet in the school minibus, which as you may know was actually the school mini. Mrs Whiffy chuckled softly to herself. 'This will wipe the smile off Curlew's face,' she muttered.

As usual, there had been new buildings added to Buttery St Crumpet school. The reception, for example, was now more like an airport check-in.

A smart young woman sat behind the desk and viewed us with a forced smile.

'I'm here to see Mr Curlew,' said Mrs Whiffy.

'He's in the theatre,' said the reception woman. 'Would you like me to page him?'

'Don't worry,' said Mrs Whiffy. 'He'll hear my footsteps.'

We pressed on down the corridor, past rooms full of neatly dressed pupils, all busily getting on with something. Some read, some painted, some practised on recorders, some hammered keyboards in the Star Wars computer suite. But the real action was going on in the Julian Plummet Theatre, which was like a nest full of worker ants, shifting scenery, tuning violins, and stepping out dance routines. Mr Curlew sat in the middle of it all, like the king of the jungle after a particularly satisfying chew on a zebra.

'Mildred!' he boomed, seeing us. 'To what do I owe this unexpected pleasure?'

Mrs Whiffy took one of the posters I'd been lugging, and handed it to her great rival. 'I'd like you to put up some of these, please,' she said.

Mr Curlew studied the poster:

DOGSBOTTOM VILLAGE SCHOOL PRESENTS

PETER PAN

BY J.M. BARRIE

ADAPTED FOR CHILDREN BY LOTTIE POPSOCK

MAY 1–3, 7P.M.

IN THE SCHOOL HALL THEATRE

directed by Redvers Grunt
assistant director Mildred Whiffy, B.Ed.

'The best school play you will see this year
BAR NONE'—Dogsbottom Governors'
Newsletter

'May the first?' said Mr Curlew. 'But . . . that's the day our play starts.'

'Is it?' said Mrs Whiffy. 'What a coincidence!'

For a moment I thought Mr Curlew's smile might fade, but he merely shrugged. 'Ah well,' he said. 'Not to worry.'

This threw Mrs Whiffy. 'Not to worry?' she

said. 'I think you should be very worried!'

'And why is that?' asked Mr Curlew, still with a confident smile.

'Because *my* play,' replied Mrs Whiffy, 'will be performed by the former pupils of the Gertrude Mancini School of Dance, Drama, and the Performing Arts!'

Mr Curlew raised his eyebrows. 'You've got *those* pupils?' he asked.

'I certainly have!' replied Mrs Whiffy.

'But . . .' began Mr Curlew, '. . . haven't you heard?'

'Heard what?' replied Mrs Whiffy.

'Why they were thrown out?' said Mr Curlew.

Suddenly Mrs Whiffy didn't look so confident.

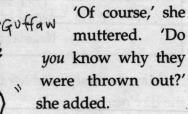

'Of course,' she muttered. 'Do *you* know why they were thrown out?' she added.

Mr Curlew made no reply. He broke into a gentle laugh, which built and built until it became the most unnerving guffaw. 'I'll tell you what, Mildred!' he cried. 'Give me all your posters! I'll put the lot up!' He then laughed even louder, and for all I know, was still laughing as the school minibus set off in a squeal of burning rubber.

Mr Tomsky on His Knees and My Nose Nearly Grows a Foot

Mrs Whiffy was very tetchy after her meeting with Mr Curlew. 'That Curlew's just trying to wind me up!' she hissed.

'I'm not so sure, Miss,' I said. 'After all, we never *did* find out why the stage kids got kicked out.'

'Whose side are you on?' rasped Mrs Whiffy.

'Just trying to see all sides, Miss,' I replied. 'No need to get a strop on.'

'How dare you talk to your headteacher like that!' roared Mrs Whiffy.

'Come off it, Miss,' I replied. 'This is Bernie you're talking to.'

Mrs Whiffy buttoned her lip. Ever since I'd saved the school from being shut down, she'd been in my pocket.

'*Anyway*,' snapped Mrs Whiffy, 'I have every reason to get a strop on. The show is on in three weeks, and *you still haven't made Peter Pan fly!*'

This was a sudden change of subject, and one I wasn't prepared for.

'I'm working on it,' I mumbled.

'You're working too slowly!' snapped Mrs Whiffy. 'I want to see that boy fly tomorrow!'

'All right, all right,' I replied. 'He'll fly.'

That evening, as I watched the rehearsal, I racked my brains for new ideas. I pictured the giant magnet, the slingshot, the row of powerful hairdryers, and the trained albatross. None of them seemed very practical.

Then I noticed something. Miles Black, as usual, was wearing all black, and as he crossed the stage in front of a black curtain, you could hardly see him.

This gave me an idea . . .

. . . yes, it might just work . . .

I went back home and looked out some black clothes. Big black clothes, large enough to fit Mr Tomsky. I found some old black jogging bottoms which Dad used to wear before Mum got rid of him. I found a baggy black jumper which Mum wore while she had a bun called Bernie in her oven. I found black socks, black gloves, and finally a black balaclava. I'm not sure where the balaclava came from. Maybe a burglar left it.

Next morning I sought out Mr Tomsky and explained my plan to him. Mr Tomsky was not keen to get involved, till I mentioned the strange disappearance of Mrs Whiffy's aniseed balls, and asked whether he might just know something about it. Mr Tomsky's tune quickly changed. He agreed to be at the hall at four, although this did *not* mean he knew anything about the missing aniseed balls.

Mrs Whiffy was awaiting me at the rehearsal. 'So,' she said. 'Is it done?'

'He flies today,' I replied.

At this point Mr Tomsky arrived at the hall. As instructed, he had changed into the black jumper and jogging bottoms, black socks, black gloves, and black balaclava. He did look a bit like a burglar, to be honest, but it would all make sense shortly.

'Right, Mr Tomsky,' I said. 'Go up on stage, next to Peter Pan, and get down on all fours.'

'Mr Tomsky can't be Nana!' protested Redvers. 'He's too big!'

'Mr Tomsky is not a dog,' I replied. 'All will be revealed shortly.'

Mr Tomsky did as instructed. Just as I planned, he was all but invisible in front of the black curtain.

'Now, Larry,' I said to Peter Pan. 'You stand on top of him.'

Mr Tomsky immediately protested, as did Larry, but I held my ground. 'I promise you,' I said, 'this will work.'

Larry gingerly stepped on to Mr Tomsky's back. Mr Tomsky gave a groan and cried, 'Watch my lumbago!' Larry jittered and wobbled and struggled to balance, holding his arms out like a tightrope-walker.

'That's it, Larry,' I said. 'Like you've got wings.'

Larry got his balance and Mr Tomsky muttered a few foul oaths.

'Now crawl, Mr Tomsky!' I cried.

'What's that?' said Mr Tomsky. 'I can't hear a thing with this balaclava on!'

'Crawl!' I cried again.

'Oh,' said Mr Tomsky. With a painful sigh, he set off across the stage, with Larry hanging on for dear life above, waggling his arms like a mad surfer.

'It's working!' I cried.

Redvers shook his head. 'Nice idea, Bernadette,' he said, 'but we can still see Mr Tomsky's face.'

Unfortunately this was true. Mr Tomsky's face showed up like a big red tomato against the black background.

I had to think fast.

'I've got it!' I cried. 'Stop, Mr Tomsky!'

'Eh?' said Mr Tomsky.

'Stop!' I cried.

Mr Tomsky stopped. 'Can't hear a thing with this balaclava on,' he repeated.

'Take the balaclava off,' I instructed.

'Thank heavens for that,' said Mr Tomsky, pulling off the balaclava with one hand, while Peter Pan wobbled precariously above.

'Now put it back on,' I ordered, 'but back to front.'

'Oh, no!' cried Mr Tomsky.

'Can I smell aniseed?' I said.

Mr Tomsky shut up and put the balaclava back on as instructed. Brilliant. Now he really was invisible.

'Crawl!' I cried.

Mr Tomsky set off again. It was an absolute success. But just as I was about to raise my fist in triumph, our old caretaker made a slight but significant change of direction. Instead of heading to the far side of the stage, he was now heading for the edge of it.

'Stop, Mr Tomsky!' we all cried.

Blind as a bat and deaf as a post, Mr Tomsky crawled on.

'Jump, Larry!' we all cried.

Peter Pan, however, was frozen in panic.

Mr Tomsky was now inches from the edge.

'*Stop, Mr Tomsky!*' we bawled.

Suddenly, at this very last second, Mr Tomsky seemed to sense the danger, and pulled up like a racehorse at a fence. Peter Pan, on the other hand, sailed on. I didn't actually see him land because my eyes were closed, but I got the distinct impression he didn't enjoy it. Nor did Redvers, Taloola, or Floribel, on whom he apparently landed. When I did open my eyes,

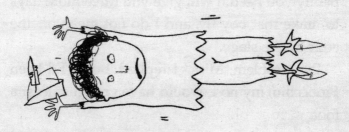

Miss Dorrit was anxiously tending to Larry, who was doing a much more convincing death scene than the one he did at football. Everyone else's eyes were fixed on me.

'Told you I'd make Peter Pan fly,' I said.

'You did this on purpose!' hissed Taloola.

'That's enough, Taloola!' snapped Mrs Whiffy. She waited till the hubbub silenced, then turned calmly to address me. 'You did this on purpose!' she roared.

I glanced anxiously at Moonbeam, who seemed to share the general view of me.

'I was just trying to do it cheap!' I blurted. 'I did have a better idea, but it would probably cost a fortune!'

The others viewed me doubtfully.

'Very well, Bernadette,' said Mrs Whiffy. 'We will go to the bank tomorrow, and borrow every penny you need. I will give you three more days to make that boy fly, and I do not mean off the edge of the stage.'

'No problem, Miss,' I replied, but if I'd been Pinocchio, my nose would have grown at least a foot.

Captain Hook Lands a Strange Fish

I would not be defeated. Inspiration would come from somewhere.

Possibly.

After two days, however, it had not arrived. I'd already been through all the ideas, and I knew none of them would work.

Then, just by chance, I went home a different way. I'd seen some dump trucks heading off down Cow Lane, so I decided to follow them. I was hoping to find some heavy industry to remind me of life back in Grosshampton.

My luck was in. There was building work going on in Cow Farm, and there in the middle of it was the most stupendous crane. I watched transfixed as it swung some big concrete blocks around on its mighty hook. How I wished I'd been that crane driver, swinging things around all day with gay abandon. It would be like being in charge of a massive metal dinosaur. I could even take it home for parties and swing my friends around for fun.

It would almost be like . . . flying.

Hmm, I thought to myself.

Yes! I thought to myself.

I didn't hang around. I marched into the farm and demanded to see the boss. I was taken to Mr Ticker, a short sweaty man in a check shirt and an armless fleece. He viewed me the way busy grown-ups usually view inconvenient brats. 'Yes?' he snapped.

'Can I borrow your crane?' I asked.

Mr Ticker gave a short laugh.

'I'll pay for it,' I added, taking out the fat wodge of notes Mrs Whiffy had entrusted me with.

'Where d'you get that from?' gasped Mr Ticker.

'No questions,' I replied. 'Can I have it or not?'

Mr Ticker glanced hungrily at the great wodge of notes, and I knew the crane was mine.

I did tell Mr Ticker a *slight* fib when I said I knew someone who could drive the crane. I didn't want to ask Mrs Whiffy because that would spoil the surprise, and I didn't want to ask Mr Tomsky because he kept running away when I got near him. I could have asked Mr Zinn, but power goes to Mr Zinn's head and if he got in a crane he'd probably try to take over the village. Mr Stains was out of the question, of course— he'd be sure to fall asleep at the wheel. That left Miss Dorrit, so next day I asked her nicely and she said she'd love to drive the crane. Although, to be exact, she didn't actually say 'drive'. What she actually said was 'play with'. It was possible Miss Dorrit thought I meant a toy crane. OK, probable.

Anyway, Mr Ticker said I could have the crane that afternoon, so just after lunch I swung into action. First I told Larry Bedstain to go to the hall and wait on the stage. Not surprisingly, Larry was nervous about this, but I assured him he could stand in the middle of the stage and nowhere near the edge. Then I explained that we would be lifting him with a large hook which he should tuck through his belt, and not to worry, because this would be perfectly safe. Larry was not convinced about this and suggested maybe we should lift Tinkerbell first, but I didn't quite hear him.

Next I asked permission from Mrs Whiffy to leave school. I explained that I had to fetch something important which would help Peter Pan to fly.

'What exactly *is* it you're fetching?' asked Mrs Whiffy.

'Captain Hook,' I replied, with a wink.

With that Miss Dorrit and I left school. Miss Dorrit was very excited and insisted we sing 'The Wheels on the Crane' all the way down Cow Lane, but when the actual crane came in sight, the song came to a sudden end.

'Oh my word,' said Miss Dorrit.

'What's the problem?' I asked. 'You can drive.'

'That,' replied Miss Dorrit, 'is *not* my Morris Minor.'

At this point Miss Dorrit looked all set to run for it, but then Mr Ticker arrived, and of course, Miss Dorrit had to be nice to him, and couldn't say no when he offered to explain how everything worked. We sat behind the controls, Miss Dorrit tried this and that, and I must say it felt great.

'Perhaps we could give it a name,' suggested Miss Dorrit. 'Then I might feel happier about it.'

'It's got a name,' I replied. 'Captain Hook.'

'A nice name,' said Miss Dorrit. 'Like Daisy.'

'Christabel Crane,' I suggested.

'Oh yes, that's lovely!' trilled Miss Dorrit. 'Perhaps I could write a children's picture book about her.'

'Don't bother,' I replied. 'Can we go now?'

'Yes, come on, Christabel!' sang Miss Dorrit. 'Oh, I do hope no one notices me.'

'Hang on,' said Mr Ticker. 'I'll just ring for the police escort.'

Unfortunately for Miss Dorrit, Mr Ticker wasn't joking. Twenty minutes later we were parading through the village with four police bikes as company, sirens wailing. It was almost as if the carnival had come to Dogsbottom. As we turned into the school, every face appeared at the window, and I just wish I could have taken a picture of their expressions.

'Oh dear, what was that bump?' asked Miss Dorrit. 'I hope we haven't gone over a hedgehog.'

I looked back. 'It's all right, Miss Dorrit,' I replied. 'It was only Mr Zinn's moped.'

'I knew I couldn't handle this thing!' complained Miss Dorrit.

'Don't call her a thing!' I protested.

'Oh!' exclaimed Miss Dorrit. 'Sorry, Christabel.'

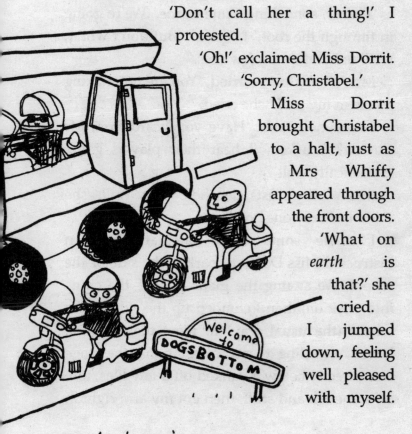

Miss Dorrit brought Christabel to a halt, just as Mrs Whiffy appeared through the front doors. 'What on *earth* is that?' she cried. I jumped down, feeling well pleased with myself.

'Meet Christabel,' I trilled. 'The crane which will make Peter Pan fly!'

'But . . . how will you get it into the hall?' asked Mrs Whiffy.

Suddenly I didn't feel so pleased. You're probably going to think I'm really stupid, but I have to admit I hadn't thought of that. However, as always, something came to me. 'We're going in through the roof,' I replied. 'But don't worry, we'll only take off a few tiles.'

Mrs Whiffy *was* worried. 'You are not making a hole in my roof!' she cried.

I remained calm. 'Have you heard from Mr Curlew?' I asked. 'I hear their play is going fantastically well.'

Mrs Whiffy's fists clenched. 'Very well,' she said. 'But only one hole!'

I made some brief calculations, then instructed Miss Dorrit to park at the side of the school. We swung the giant arm of the crane into position, then I climbed up the side of the school (the usual way) to meet the dangling hook. According to my calculations, the stage was directly below. I yanked off a few tiles, tore off some felt and stuff, then got my arm right in and punched away at some plasterboard till there was a hole big enough for the hook.

'Fire away, Miss Dorrit!' I cried.

Miss Dorrit lowered the hook through the hole I'd made, down into the bowels of the school. I yelled for Larry to get himself hooked on, but it was hard to know if he'd heard me.

'Can you feel anything, Miss Dorrit?' I asked.

'Not yet,' replied Miss Dorrit. 'This is rather fun, isn't it? It reminds me of those machines on Sandover Pier. Once I caught a real plastic key ring, and another time—' Miss Dorrit stopped.

'What's up, Miss?' I asked.

'I've got something!' cried Miss Dorrit.

'Pull up, Miss Dorrit!' I yelled.

Miss Dorrit hauled the hook back upwards; not too far mind, because we didn't want Peter Pan coming through the roof.

'Good old Christabel!' cried Miss Dorrit. 'She's done it!'

I could hardly wait to see our handiwork. I clambered down the school, sprinted through the lobby past the WALK DON'T RUN sign, and arrived gasping in the hall.

Larry was still standing on the stage, gazing hopefully upwards.

'Larry!' I cried. 'You're not flying!'

'I had noticed,' replied Larry.

'But . . . where's the hook?' I gulped.

'You tell me, Bernadette,' replied Larry.

I ran up on stage and ferreted through the curtains. No, no sign of it. But it had to be *somewhere*!

I hurried out of the hall and down the corridor, looking up all the time. Then I became aware of anxious cries coming from the classroom at the far end. I arrived half breathless to be met by a quite amazing and also disturbing sight. The whole class had stopped work and were gazing upwards with worried frowns. And there, some ten feet above the chair where he normally sat, was Mr Stains, slowly revolving on Christabel's mighty hook.

Fortunately, however, the experience had not disturbed Mr Stains's regular afternoon nap.

'Would you like to explain this, Bernadette?' asked Mrs Whiffy, who had sneaked up behind me on her sinister silent shoes.

'Er . . . it's the trial run,' I stammered. 'I'll need to make another hole.'

'Make the next one in the school garden,' said Mrs Whiffy. 'And when you've finished digging it, jump in it!'

It All Ends Dramatically

There were no more attempts to make Peter Pan fly. There were too many other important things to do, and as the big day grew closer, I slunk around school feeling more out of it than ever. For all my efforts, Moonbeam still wasn't talking to me.

And then, suddenly, the big day was tomorrow. The school was buzzing like bees with a buzz-saw, and Mrs Whiffy wore the fixed stare of a stalking cat. Up on stage, the scenery was in place, the lights had been tested, and Mr

Tomsky had practised cranking the winding-wheel which wound the curtains open and shut. Even Mr Stains was ready, though what exactly for, no one seemed to know. He was sitting at the side of the stage with a script in his hand at going-home time, and he was still there next morning, with a bit more stubble on his chin.

There were no lessons on Play Day. Miss Dorrit's classroom was transformed into the make-up room, and Mr Stains's room was full of anxious actors pacing up and down repeating their lines. As tea-time approached, every chair in school was carried to the hall, where the assistant director sorted them out into rows.

'Are you sure we'll need all these chairs, Mrs Whiffy?' asked Mr Tomsky.

'Why?' snapped Mrs Whiffy. 'What have you heard?'

'Nothing,' said Mr Tomsky. 'Except there is a play on at Buttery St—'

'There is only *one* play on tonight!' roared Mrs Whiffy.

Mr Tomsky fell silent.

'Bernadette,' ordered Mrs Whiffy. 'Get a large

sheet of card, about the size of a bungalow, and paint THIS WAY TO THE PLAY on it.'

I did as I was told. We carried the giant sign down to the school gates and set it up. One end of it poked slightly out into the road, so cars had to swerve to go round it.

'There's a fine big sign,' said Mrs Gannet from the post office.

'A fine sign for a fine play, Mrs Gannet,' said Mrs Whiffy. 'I trust we can keep a seat warm for you tonight?'

'Erm . . .' said Mrs Gannet, '. . . I'd *like* to, Mrs Whiffy, but I'm afraid I've already got tickets for another show.'

Mrs Whiffy's face frosted over. 'I see,' she said. 'And Mr Gannet?'

'Well, he's going with me, of course,' said Mrs Gannet. 'In fact, we've got quite a party going from the village.'

'Is that so,' growled Mrs Whiffy. She watched Mrs Gannet disappear then turned to me with a face like fury. 'Right, Bernadette,' she said. 'I want you, Zinn, Floss, and Tomsky to go to the potting shed and bring me the drag net.'

I really didn't like the sound of this. Mrs

Whiffy had never shown any interest in Mr Tomsky's fishing gear before. But as usual, I did as I was told, and helped the others carry the monstrous net back to the school gates, where Mrs Whiffy was now waiting with a megaphone.

'Follow me,' she ordered. With that, she set off at a quick march through the village, past the post office, the surgery, the Vipers Arms and the village hall, all the way to the village church at the top of the hill and the sign which said DOGSBOTTOM WELCOMES CAREFUL DRIVERS. At this point Mrs Whiffy instructed us to fan out across the road and unfurl the net.

'Now,' she said. 'I want you walk slowly and steadily back through the village, keeping the net tight, and do not stop unless I instruct you to do so.'

We began to walk slowly and steadily back through the village, keeping the net tight, etc., etc. Mrs Whiffy raised the megaphone to her lips.

'Earthquake warning!' she bellowed. 'Flee your buildings!'

Mrs Floss made as if to protest, but one glare silenced her. People were already hobbling and pattering out of their houses, some in their dressing-gowns, and it wasn't long before our net was almost half full.

'Earthquake warning!' yelled Mrs Whiffy. 'Indoors is the most dangerous place to be!'

We pressed on through the village, like farmers herding their cows to market. Behind us was a long row of cars parping their horns, and before us house after house was emptying. Soon just about every character from the village was in the net.

'Where are we going?' cried Mr Snapper the dentist.

'To the only safe building in Dogsbottom,' replied Mrs Whiffy. 'Dogsbottom School.'

'But I'm supposed to be going to Buttery St Crumpet!' complained Mrs Dark the potter.

'Buttery St Crumpet?' sneered Mrs Whiffy. 'At the first rumble that school will collapse like a pack of cards!'

We reached the school gates, and herded the dazed villagers up the drive and through the doors, where each was greeted by a small cube of cheese on a stick, and a plastic cup of Mrs Floss's home-made dandelion wine.

'As you may know,' said Mrs Whiffy, 'there is, fortunately, a show on tonight.'

Mrs Whiffy handed out programmes for *Peter Pan*, and guided the villagers into the hall, where, still dazed, they took their seats. Soon the hall was full to the brim. Showtime had finally arrived.

'Super,' said Mrs Whiffy, rubbing her hands gleefully. 'Now all we need are the actors.'

I followed Mrs Whiffy up into the wings of the stage and out of the side door. This was the shortcut to Miss Dorrit's room, where the cast was putting on costumes and make-up. But the moment we opened Miss Dorrit's door, we could see that something was wrong. The actors were all sitting very still and silent, and their faces were a pale shade of green.

'Miss Dorrit!' cried Mrs Whiffy. 'What have you done? I told you to use peachy cream for their faces!'

'I never made them up that colour, Mrs Whiffy!' pleaded Miss Dorrit. 'They just . . . went that colour!'

Mrs Whiffy turned on Larry Bedstain. 'What's the matter with you?' she shrilled.

'Sick,' murmured Larry.

'Sick?' repeated Mrs Whiffy. 'What was it? Mrs Floss's stew?'

'Stage sick,' burbled Larry.

'Always . . . get like this,' mumbled Floribel.

Mrs Whiffy began to look very worried indeed. 'You mean . . .' she gasped, '. . . you've got stage fright?'

'Don't say that!' cried Miles.

'Now I'm even more sick!' cried Larry.

'It's impossible!' cried Mrs Whiffy. 'You're old

troupers! You've been on stage thousands of times!'

'No, we haven't,' mumbled Taloola.

'We haven't been on stage once,' added Floribel.

'But . . . you went to stage school!' blurted Mrs Whiffy.

'Till they kicked us out,' replied Larry.

'Why do you think they kicked us out?' added Miles.

A look of horror came over Mrs Whiffy. She shivered a little, as if remembering the manic cackle of Mr Curlew. 'Where's Redvers?' she demanded.

'Gone home, Miss,' grunted Miles.

'He always does it,' added Floribel.

Mrs Whiffy's horror grew. 'But . . . you've got to go on stage!' she cried.

No one moved.

'I'll give you money!' cried Mrs Whiffy.

Still no one moved. Then, at last, Larry stirred. 'Hand me Peter's hat,' he murmured.

Mrs Whiffy seized the hat in question and handed it to Larry. 'That's the attitude, Larry!' she said. 'Show us what you can do!'

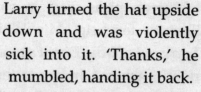

Larry turned the hat upside down and was violently sick into it. 'Thanks,' he mumbled, handing it back.

Mrs Whiffy turned a shade of purple which clashed badly with the green faces all around. 'Has no one got the guts to go on stage?' she roared.

Moonbeam shyly raised her hand. She was sitting in the far corner, hardly noticed in all the drama. 'Please, Miss,' she said. 'I'm all right.' Sure enough, she was peachy white, if a little shaky.

'Well done, Moonbeam,' said Mrs Whiffy. 'At least you're not a snivelling yellow-belly.'

'But I've got no one to act with, Miss,' said Moonbeam.

'Yes you have,' said Mrs Whiffy. 'Larry is going to act.'

Larry shook his green head vigorously. 'No, Miss!' he pleaded.

103

Larry's pleas were in vain. Calling on Mr Tomsky for help, Mrs Whiffy bodily carried Larry out of Miss Dorrit's room, through the back door of the hall and on to the stage. Moonbeam hurried after, closely followed by me.

'Open the curtain,' cried Mrs Whiffy, 'and let the show begin!'

'Are you sure this is wise, Mrs Whiffy?' asked Mr Tomsky.

'Once I was afraid to swim,' replied Mrs Whiffy. 'My dear mother threw me in at the deep end and my fear vanished.'

'You swam?' asked Mr Tomsky.

'No,' replied Mrs Whiffy. 'I was unconscious in the hospital. But it was still the right thing to do. Now open the curtain!'

Mr Tomsky turned the great winding-wheel, the curtains came apart, and the audience was treated to its first sight of Peter Pan, minus his hat. Larry blinked into the light, opened his mouth as if to speak, and promptly fell into a dead faint. There was a moment of awful suspense. Then, once again, it was Moonbeam who came to the rescue. She rushed on to the stage, grabbed Larry's hand,

and cried out, 'Is there a doctor in the house?'

The crowd were silent. They weren't sure if this was all part of the play. In that moment, I suddenly knew what I must do. Without further ado I followed Moonbeam on to the stage, calling out, 'What is the problem, Nurse Tinkerbell?'

Moonbeam was a little shocked. 'Don't mess about,' she said. 'He's fainted.'

'I certainly won't mess about, Nurse Tinkerbell,' I replied. 'You clear his airways and I'll check his pulse.'

Rather uncertainly, Moonbeam adjusted Larry's head. It was something she'd done a hundred times, though generally with a fluffy toy. At this point Larry began to come round. 'What's going on?' he mumbled.

'Just shut up and lie still!' I hissed.

'Shall I . . . check his blood pressure?' asked Moonbeam. Now that Larry was awake, and we were stuck there on stage, she had obviously decided to make a go of it.

'Yes, do that, Nurse Tinkerbell,' I replied. 'And while you're at it, check mine, cos I've been working non-stop since Tuesday.'

There was a laugh, a single laugh, out in the

crowd. This hyped us up no end. Our little scene picked up steam, and now that they knew it was supposed to be funny, the whole audience began to laugh. It was like being picked up on a great big breaker. Soon we were surfing on it for all we were worth, playing out the scenes we'd done a hundred times, but a thousand times better. We even dragged old Tomsky on as the hospital porter, and he was brilliant, although I'm not sure he realized we were acting.

I don't know how long we were up there. It was a magical place under those bright lights, with an invisible beast lurking in the shadows, a big friendly beast which went *oooo* and *ahhh* and *hahaha*. I felt like I'd stepped out of time, into ghost time, and the stage was like a warm bath I wanted to float in for ever. But all good things have to come to an end, and when the nail scissors were finally removed from Larry's appendix, it was obviously time to finish. The curtain closed, the applause rang out, and we ran out again to milk it. As I bowed for the tenth time, I held my hand out towards Moonbeam, and after a moment's hesitation, she took it.

The Final Plastic Toast

Doctors and Fairies played to a packed hall for all three nights, although it was actually the same audience each night. After the first night they came of their own free will, and would have kept coming for another month if that was possible. The thing was, *Doctors and Fairies* was different each night, and at least ten times better than *Joseph and His Amazing Stain-Resistant Jimjams*.

We never knew exactly how many people went to Buttery St Crumpet's play, because Mr Curlew wouldn't say. He hung up every time

Mrs Whiffy rang him, which was about once an hour. Word was, he was looking for another job as a librarian or an assistant in a quiet museum in the Outer Hebrides.

On the last night of the show, Mrs Whiffy invited us into her room for a plastic beaker of weak orange squash. It was her way of saying thank you. I sat next to Moonbeam, feeling that special feeling you get when you're with your best friend, like you're strong and complete and everything's as it should be. Moonbeam had accepted my apologies, all five hundred of them. She'd even begun to understand why I was so nasty, which was hard for Moonbeam, because she didn't have one bit of nastiness in her.

'To our fantastic success!' said Mrs Whiffy, raising her plastic beaker.

'To our fantastic success!' we repeated, trying to clink our beakers together, which just made a soft *duk* sound. But there was still one thing getting in the way of true happiness.

'Mrs Whiffy,' I said, 'what will happen to the new kids?'

Mrs Whiffy shook her head sadly. 'I'm afraid,' she said, 'they will have to find another school.'

I tried not to smile. 'Why, Mrs Whiffy?' I asked.

'They are not suitable,' replied Mrs Whiffy, 'for a school of this type.'

'This type?' I repeated. 'What type is that?'

Mrs Whiffy smiled broadly, which did not happen often. 'I've . . . er . . . had a new sign done for the school,' she said. With that, she drew a large metal sign from beneath her desk:

THE MILDRED WHIFFY SCHOOL OF DANCE, DRAMA, AND THE PERFORMING ARTS

'What do you think?' she asked.

'Er . . .' said Moonbeam.

'Er . . .' said Mr Tomsky.

'Earthquake warning!' I cried. 'Flee the building!'

CAVAN COUNTY LIBRARY

Jon Blake was born at the age of 0 in Berkshire and brought up in Southampton. At the age of 12 Jon decided to become a writer, and sure enough, six years later, he was a furniture salesman. After going to college he decided again to become a writer (or possibly a punk rock star). Then he became a teacher. That didn't last long, and in 1986 Jon really did get a novel published called *Yatesy's Rap*. Since then he has written over 40 books, been shortlisted for the Children's Book Award and a Writers' Guild TV award, and won a BBC Talent competition for radio comedy.

Jon now lives in Cardiff and his hobbies include gardening and overthrowing society. He also makes a lot of loud music and still intends to become a punk rock star, preferably before he gets his pension.

How the mayhem began . . .

Oh no! I never meant for this to happen! All I wanted was for Mum to send me to the school in the big town, but somehow I've managed to mess things up. Now all the other pupils have gone and I'm the only one left . . .

It's hard being the only pupil. How am I supposed to be the football captain, goalie, and top scorer all at the same time? It's crazy! And the teachers are no help at all—in fact, I think they're all starting to go a little bit mad . . .

ISBN 0 19 275396 7

The madness continues . . .

I tell you, things at Dogsbottom School have gone from bad to worse. OK, I'm not the only pupil any more, but you should see the rest of them. Goody-goodies, or what?

Now Mrs Whiffy wants new stuff for the school —but the only way to get it is with a Problem Pupil grant. How is she going to make problem pupils out of this lot of teachers' pets? Looks as if she needs my help again . . .

ISBN 0 19 275394 0